Richard Scarry's
ABC'S

A GOLDEN BOOK • NEW YORK
Western Publishing Company, Inc., Racine, Wisconsin 53404

It is a lovely summer evening. Charlie Chipmunk has invited Big Hilda Hippo to dinner outdoors. But Charlie can't decide what to feed her.

Will you help Charlie pick the proper ABC foods to feed Big Hilda?

A a

Would you feed her
an **alligator**? Or an **apple**?
Which would you feed her?

Watch your tail,
Charlie! **Alligators**
can bite!

Would a **bed** be good
to eat? Or a **banana**?

B b

Have you ever seen
a hippo eat a **bed**?

Cc

Would Hilda like to eat a **carrot**?

Or a **clock**?
If she ate a **clock**,
she might always
say "Tick-tock."

Would you serve her a **doughnut** with a hole?

Dd

Or a **drum**?

Do you eat a **drum** with a fork or a spoon?

Do you think she would like an **egg**? Or a train **engine**?

Ee

Which would you prefer?

Ff

Is a **fiddle** good to eat?

Or **fudge**?

Would you give
Hilda **grapes**?

Gg

Or a **glove**?

If she eats one **glove**,
do you think she should
eat another so that she
has a pair?

Hh

Would she like to eat a **hat**? Or a **hot dog**?

Do you put mustard on the **hats** you eat?

Ii

I know Hilda would like some **ice cream**.

Wouldn't you like strawberry **ice cream** with a cherry on top?

Jj

Do you think Hilda would like to eat a **jeep**?

Or would she like some **jam**?

What does a **jeep** taste like? Does it taste like **jam**?

Kk

How would Hilda like
a nice ripe **kite**?

Or do you think
a candy **kiss** is nicer?

Ll

Is Hilda hungry enough to eat all this **laundry**?

Maybe she would like some **lemonade** instead.

Mm

Shall we feed her a **mop**?
Or a great big slice of **melon**?

Oh, dear! Hilda
sat on the **melon**.

Do you think she would like to chew on a **nest**?

Nn

Or would she rather have a **nut**?

Shall we feed her some nice fresh **overalls**?

Oo

Or an **orange**?

P p

How about a nice **pink package** to munch on?

Or a **peach**?

Hilda should check what's in the **package**. It might taste awful!

Q q

Do you eat a **quilt** while sitting up or lying down?

I don't think Hilda wants to eat a **quilt**!

Rr

Is Hilda hungry enough to eat a **refrigerator**?

Or would she prefer a **roast** of beef?

Ss

Now, shall we give
Hilda a **stove** with
pepper on it?

Or a **sandwich**
with **salt** on it?

Termites are little insects that like to eat **tables** and anything made of wood.

Would Hilda like to eat a **table** or a **tomato**?

Wow! Look at that **termite** eat the **table**!

T t

Uu

Anyone who would try
to eat an **umbrella** would
be very silly.

Please don't feed an
umbrella to Hilda.
It would taste awful.

Instead, feed Hilda her **vitamins**.

Vv

Ww

She will need a glass of **water** to wash them down.

X x

Hilda has finished her dinner. She puts her knife and fork on her plate. They look like the letter **X.**

Y y

Hilda is too tired to play with her **yo-yo.** She opens her mouth wide and **yawns.**

Zz

Hilda is so sleepy after such a big meal. Off to sleep she goes. **ZZZZZZZZZZ!**

Charlie is tired after serving Hilda her proper ABC foods. Have a nice nap, Charlie. **ZZZZZ!**

Hilda wants to thank you and Charlie for feeding her. Can you name the things she has eaten, as well as those she hasn't eaten?

A   B   C   D   E   F   G

H   I   J   K   L   M   N

O   P   Q   R   S   T

U   V   W   X   Y   Z

If you are hungry tonight before you go to bed, eat something. But never, never eat your bed!